Sweet & Sour

Short Stories,

Sweet and Sour Fiction

by

Jane Palmer

Dodo Books

Stories

FLORENCE FOR TEA

It was difficult to move silently through the litter of last year's twigs in the oversized Wellingtons borrowed from the zoo. The vet carrying a case containing tranquillizing darts and a gun had not expected to be dragooned into manoeuvres which would have exhausted the Territorial Army: she had merely expected to look at the recurring rash on the ear of an elderly lemur. Nothing had been mentioned about stunning a large arboreal primate with a sweet tooth.

'For pity's sake!' the vet complained to the nearest zoo attendant. 'She's harmless. Why couldn't you just leave some food out and let her come back in her own time?'

'Head Keeper don't want the press to pick it up.'

'And he thinks a battalion of beaters ploughing through the countryside isn't going to attract attention?'

'What if she reaches the village? Just hope there's no ice cream van doing its rounds. You know what our Florence would do for an ice cream, don't you.'

The vet said nothing. She knew only too well what Florence would do for something sweet. It was a wonder she could still get off the ground.

The late spring air was warm, the sun at its height and the birds busy defending their territories and feeding young.

Monica slammed down a handful of cutlery onto the garden table as though declaring war with the plates stacked at its other end.

'Of course we'll come and see you every now and then,' her sons had promised. 'And we'll bring all the family. Be prepared!'

So Monica left her luxury yacht, bought a cottage in the country, and a sturdy garden table which could seat twenty. And how often had that table been used? Three times. Once for the vicarage's garden fete and twice by the fuchsia society. Now the grass underneath it was dying.

As she brought out a strawberry cheesecake and plate of cress sandwiches the once mistress of her own destiny considered donating the table to the village hall. But there was one last purpose it was going to serve before that. Monica went back to collect the chocolate éclairs and Black Forest gateau, which she dumped against the large platter of cheese scones that were sent rolling across the lacy tablecloth it had taken weeks to crochet.

Of course, one o'clock was rather early to serve high tea, but as no one was coming to eat it the time was academic. The food could have been frozen if Monica had been prepared to allow confectionery to take up the space intended for the lovingly grown beans, peas and cauliflowers surrounded by a rabbit proof fence garlanded with spinning bottle tops to scare off the pigeons. Another exercise in futility; the wildlife here was relentless. At least you could shoot sharks menacing your snorkelling passengers and no one would have been any the wiser. Oh, how she wished to be back at sea.

At last the table was filled with cutlery, crockery, glasses, sandwiches, sweets, savouries, cold soup, flower displays and serviettes; yet something was still missing. Yes, of course - people!

Monica tossed a few chairs roughly into position and sat glowering at the spread. The vibrations she sent out deterred even the pigeons from coming down to try their luck. Perhaps she should invite some of those contractors waiting to fell the nearby local wood

so they could build a slip road? No, they were trying
to lower the value of her property and no one in the
village would speak to her again if they saw the
footprints of their muddy boots on her path. She
could, of course, have invited some neighbours.
Unfortunately all the locals here did was grumble
about a world they knew nothing of, people on
benefits in general, and luscious Lulu up Brook's
Alley in particular. At least that woman took the
trouble to look in the mirror before she stepped
outside. Monica would certainly have allowed her on
the luxury 55 foot yacht, regardless of how she had
raised the fare. And Lulu would have added a bit of
sparkle to her table, though Monica would have
probably ended up branded as her madam or maid.

There was nothing else for it; the only way now
was death by dessert.

Without a second glance at the sandwiches,
Monica ploughed straight into the Black Forest
gateau. Spooning her way through the cherry laden
chocolate sponge and cream, she gazed up absently at
the line of flimsy huts perched precariously in the
trees. Strange birds, their plumage braided with
beads, had nested there and only came down to collect
the tins of food donated by appreciative villagers. Now
the wood was virtually deserted while everyone
waited for the Transport Minister's final decision.

As Monica automatically swallowed cake she
noticed the flash of a mirrored skirt in one of the tree
houses and recognised the red velvet jacket which had
been parcelled up with a few other things for the
weekly collection by local sympathisers. They were
worn by the scrawny pair in danger of having a
cuckoo chick push them from their nest.

Monica waved. A thin hand waved back. She
raised the plate of gateau and beckoned them to join

her. The response was immediate. The solitary protesters scrambled down a knotted rope and bounced through the leaf litter, barely giving Monica time to set two places at the table.

The couple wriggled through the yew hedge and self consciously darted towards the table like unsure squirrels. Unused to garden parties, they hesitated at the sight of the incongruously deserted banquet.

'Hi. My name's Monica. I recommend the cucumber and fennel soup for starters, but if you're really hungry, plough into anything you like.'

Now they were at eye level, Monica noticed that the leanness of her guests was due to emaciation, not youth. Far from being teenagers, it was obvious that they were in their late thirties. Despite their weather-beaten skin, these protesters had that innate delicacy often found in the morally aware, as well as an otherworldliness which would have obliged them to defend the Asteroid Belt from mining companies.

The woman plucked open her serviette with birdlike fingers. 'This is really very generous of you. Are you sure we're not intruding?'

'Intrude all you like. My name is Monica, though my crew used to call me Captain Blood.'

The young woman made a gallant effort not to look worried. Decent food was too much of an imperative that moment. 'My name's Euphan. My friend is called Tristan.'

Tristan's mouth was already full of cheese scone and he spluttered his appreciation.

Monica swallowed the last of her gateau and, regretting it, next filled her plate with cress sandwiches.

'Where will you go when the decision for this road scheme is settled?'

Tristan swallowed. 'Probably on to the next one, but we're starting to win y'know. May not be many more after this.'

'Amen to that.' Monica doubted it. Living in a village she was obliged to have a car, but still preferred her luxury yacht which had ferried the wealthy from port to port, or circled the coast with billionaires' mistresses, and their pets which would have otherwise gone into quarantine. With a second mate, six crew, steward and cook to order about, Captain Blood had been on her very own highway of life. What was she now? A grandmother who had just spent all week cooking for a family who suddenly decided they had something better to do.

Euphan sensed the angry cloud hanging over her host. 'This is so good of you, but will there be enough left for your guests?'

Monica planted glasses of apple juice before them. 'You are my guests.'

Euphan mouthed a noncommittal, 'Oh,' and thought it safest to just carry on nibbling her scone.

Tristan was too immersed in gastric gratification to notice any tension. 'Of course, we could always try Greenpeace again. I've got nautical experience and can handle a dinghy.'

Monica swallowed half a sandwich prematurely. 'Are you mad!'

'Sudden ambushes on ships dumping toxic waste are very effective.'

'The only sudden thing about getting under falling drums filled with toxic waste is death.'

Euphan rushed in to agree. 'I keep telling him that. And he's far too old. They wouldn't let him do it.'

'Shouldn't think so either.' Monica tossed a slice of flan onto his plate. Tristan cautiously eased a piece of it away with his fork. 'It's vegetarian - filled with nuts and free range eggs.' That was a concession to her youngest grandson, the only child in her self interested brood who actually thought about what he was eating. The carnivores and bullies would soon knock that out of him if she couldn't persuade him to run away to sea first. The sea... A dreamy expression crossed Monica's face as she recalled the changing ocean skies, uninhabited tropical shores, and the thrill of watching whales breach in greeting.

She finished her plate of cress sandwiches and reached for the éclairs. 'How long were you at sea?'

'Ten years. Six as a merchant seaman and two on an oil rig supply ship.'

'Can you read a chart?'

'Was working towards a pilot's licence when I met Euphan,' Tristan explained.

Euphan washed down her scone with apple juice before taking a slice from the flan Monica offered. 'I wanted Tristan to carry on, but he insisted on joining me at my first bypass protest.'

He shrugged. 'Well, what would there be to come back to if someone doesn't make a stand now? The country will soon be overwhelmed by fumes. Small wonder the land is repeatedly flooded when it's covered in so much tarmac.'

'Ocean's not so clean,' Monica warned. 'The North Atlantic Drift doesn't only push a warm current our way. You wouldn't believe some of the things I've seen float past on the high seas. Then there's the other sort of filth that has to be seen off with guns.'

Euphan's jaw dropped. 'You've actually had to fight off pirates?'

'Once we mounted the machine gun on the stern they didn't bother us. You'd think I'd used the same ploy on my family by the way they keep changing course to avoid me.'

By the expressions of her guests, they were taking
on board how Monica had earned the name of Captain
Blood. But, what the hell! She had every right to be
belligerent and took a large bite of her éclair.

'It's a shame ... all this food,' Euphan
commiserated.

Monica was not a defeatist. 'Plough on, children. I
have indigestion tablets and live yoghurt waiting in
the kitchen.'

After a few more minutes of serious gluttony, there
was a penetrating 'Cooeee!' from the front garden.

'I'm out the back, Gussie!' Monica shouted in mid
swallow, nearly choking on an almond slice.

The visitor had already started her side of the
conversation before coming into view. 'Just thought
I'd pop round before everyone arriv-'

The ample woman stopped in surprise as she came
round the rose trellis, though the hem of her
voluminous, flowery gown kept travelling a little
longer and described a ripple of organza violets in the
breeze.

She cautiously approached, voice lowered. 'What
happened?'

'Both my little shits decided to take their revolting
broods to EuroDisney instead. Something about a
special offer for the simpering and sub human.'

'Oh dear.' Gussie sat down opposite Tristan and
Euphan, giving them a discrete wave of recognition.

'Grab a plate, Gussie. We have leagues to go yet.'

'You'll make yourself bad,' she declared
unconvincingly as she placed the plastic bag she was
clutching on the table. 'Brought your basil. Like me to
pot it up for you?'

'Later. I know you would prefer to dive in from the
high board.'

Gussie gingerly took a plate. 'You know I'm trying to lose weight.'

'You're always trying to lose weight. It never works, so why worry about it now?'

'Just a little, then.' Gussie cut a sliver of cheesecake and poured a few drops of single cream over it.

Monica smiled to herself. Her friend had known what cutlery was for before she could say 'jam trifle' and the subsequent delicacies which hadn't passed those poppy red lips weren't worth tasting.

'Actually,' Gussie began, but was unable to resist swallowing a mouthful of cheesecake before going on. 'That friend of my mother is visiting. You said you would like to meet him.'

'Is he hungry?' Monica hesitated. 'What friend is that?'

'You know. Dorian. He used to be a steward on the QE2.'

Monica's crusade against her waistline was momentarily sidetracked. 'Was? You never said he retired?'

'He decided to go into business with a neighbour. They run a waste recycling company in the East End.'

What limited knowledge Monica had about the QE2, being a steward on it didn't seem the best qualification for going into the waste disposal business. 'Tristan here wants to ram ships dumping waste with a rubber dingy.'

'I know, dear, but don't pay any attention to him. He's far too skinny for that sort of thing.' Gussie's plump arms broke the cover of her organza sleeves to reach for a cheese scone, some cucumber and fennel soup and a handful of bread sticks. 'I told Dorian to pop along if I wasn't back in ten minutes?'

'Fine. Pass me the mango chutney will you, Euphan.' Monica decided to follow Gussie's savoury example and scooped several dollops onto a cheese scone.

Gussie looked at the selection of confectionary on the plates surrounding her friend. 'Aren't you taking things a little out of sequence?'

'The only thing I took out of sequence was trying to raise a family before I was seventy.'

'Don't be absurd. Nobody could produce a family after that age, even with the wonders of modern medical science,' Gussie admonished, her tone having the edge of the herbalist remembering what the Witchfinder General did to her forebears.

Trust her friend to miss the point. 'I would be prepared to live with the frustration.'

'So now you regret selling the yacht.'

Monica gave her a sly, enigmatic glance over her glass of apple juice. The look reminded Tristan that he was sitting at the table of a captain who kept a machine gun in the hold.

No more was said. There were places even Gussie's open toed court shoes dare not tread.

After sampling something from every plate within reach, even her appetite flagged. Euphan and Tristan had to loosen their belts and Monica felt too bloated to get up and fetch the indigestion tablets. Despite that, more than two thirds of the spread still remained when Dorian appeared. The effete 50-something may have been in the waste recycling business, yet wore a batik shirt and white trousers as though his natural habitat was the deck of a cruise liner.

He came over with a sprightly step to shake Monica's hand. 'I'm so pleased to meet you. I've always wondered what it would be like to serve on a luxury yacht like yours.'

'It wasn't the QE2. You needed a decent sense of balance.'

'What sort of people hired your vessel?'

If this guest was going to talk shop, his narrow waistline was obliged to pay the penalty, so Monica handed him a plate and waved him to a seat.

'You also needed to phone Interpol before taking on clients. Grab some food.'

'Well thank you, I did miss lunch.' Dorian deftly cut a piece of flan and dressed it with green salad as though about to serve it to an archduke. 'Were your clients really that suspect?'

'About every other one. My yacht could have taken them into international waters before the police knew the bank had been robbed.' Fond recollections brightened Monica's mood. 'Never got caught out, though. The nearest I came to ferrying a villain was when the best mate of my useless, eldest son needed passage to Calais to collect a van load of wine.'

Gussie piled some salad onto her plate. 'There you go again. Your family can't be that bad. You were the one to bring them up after all... Well, before you left them with their father and took to the high seas.'

'They were over 21. I was entitled to.'

Tristan had also gone to sea to escape a life of emotional entanglement and appreciated Monica's reluctance to discuss hers. 'What was the name of your yacht?' he asked.

'Sibella. You wouldn't have seen it when you were working the oil rig run.' Monica turned to Dorian. 'Why did you leave the QE2?'

He sighed. 'They needed younger legs and higher heels. Everyone around me was half my age. Why did you give up the sea?'

Monica was silent for a while. 'No idea. Must have been mad.'

Silence once again descended. By this time Monica was so full she stopped to watch Dorian eat with elegant enthusiasm and the others, also full up, pick at morsels. Eventually a comfortable wave of oneness descended over the company, almost as though they were linking hands in some empathic ether.

None of them had been expecting the rustling in the branches of the old oak overhanging the table.

Monica gave the tree a cursory glance. 'Bloody squirrels. They've smelt the hazelnut flan.' She poured herself some spring water. 'Who else is going to finish all this food? It's a pity you wouldn't have a freezer, Gussie. '

'I prefer to dry my herbs.'

'Freezers are very handy. You can live out of them for ages.'

'It's people like you who put rural shops out of business.'

'Spent too long at sea. What you couldn't purchase by the hundredweight wasn't worth taking on board.'

The words were hardly out of Monica's mouth when a huge, hairy body of muscle and fat crashed onto the far end of the table. Plates, glasses, cakes, sandwiches, scones and cutlery did a brief mid air ballet before landing like jackstones on the lacy tablecloth. The gathering stared in disbelief at the doleful sack of blubber covered with long orange hair.

Gussie took a deep breath. 'I say, isn't that an orang-utan?'

Monica opened her mouth, but all that came out was an infantile squeak. Euphan, at one with all Mother Nature's creatures, rescued a cream cake and gingerly edged her way down the table to the mournful heap sitting on several éclairs, a Victoria sponge and flower display. Fixing her with a steady gaze, the orang-utan delicately accepted the offering.

Jutting out her elastic lower lip, Florence dropped the cake into her mouth and, without bothering to masticate, swallowed it.

Encouraged, Gussie sliced a large portion of Black Forest gateau and followed suit.

'Steady on, we'll never get rid of the thing if you encourage it.' Only after the words had come out did Monica realise how absurd she sounded.

'Well she seems very friendly.' Gussie was obviously entranced by the visitor. 'And she does have a sweet tooth.'

'Try her with a cheese scone.'

Florence popped the offered morsel into her mouth, slowly masticated, swallowed, and then pulled a face which could only have meant two out of ten. Euphan quickly gave the orang-utan another cream cake.

'Think all that sweet stuff is good for it, Eu?' asked Tristan.

Monica grunted. 'When you're that size, who's going to argue?'

Dorian pulled out his glasses and peered thoughtfully at the ape. 'An old Chinese sailor I knew had an animal like that on his junk. Used to be very helpful with the rigging.'

Monica loaded a platter with éclairs, cream buns and gateau.

The orang-utan gazed at the pile of cakes as though having a near death experience in some confectionery heaven and a vengeful god was about to haul her back to reality. Ponderously, she lifted each delicacy and posted them into her capacious stomach.

'Think we ought to phone someone?' suggested Tristan.

'Let her have fun first,' said Gussie. 'She'll probably have the rest of her life in some enclosure to burn it off.'

The thought of being confined made Monica shudder.

'Alright?' asked Gussie.

'What am I doing here?'

'Playing grandma to a phantom family when you should be plying the Caribbean,' Gussie scolded. 'What did you have to go and sell the yacht for?'

Monica gave her that sly, sideways glance again.

'You did sell the yacht didn't you?' her friend demanded, not believing she would have kept something like that from her.

'That's what the boys told me to do. They would be a darn sight more attentive if they thought I was liable to take off again.'

'And them expecting to inherit a small fortune from its sale. Really Monica, that's dishonest.'

Everyone burst out laughing. Florence paused to cast a bemused glance at them before proceeding to graze from the surrounding plates.

Monica sat back and chewed a breadstick, the only thing her stomach could make room for. 'I rented the yacht out to a small cruise line. The lease is up for renewal in four weeks.'

'You know something,' Gussie sighed hopefully, 'I've always wanted to go on a cruise.'

'Sibella will need a cook. Any good at cordon bleu?'

For a successful waste disposal merchant, Dorian was paying unusually keen interest. 'What about clients?'

'Had at least a dozen contact me since Christmas.'

'So all you need now is a crew?'

Tristan gave Euphan an appealing look.

But Monica was concentrating on the orang-utan. 'Pity there isn't any rigging.'

SOULS REMEMBERED

It was that time of year again: the High Street filled with fairy lights, brass instruments blasting out Christmas carols (badly), and shoppers squandering the last of the money provided by the friendly, neighbourhood loan shark.

Moon didn't mind the holly, ivy or mistletoe so much; it was the celebration of a virgin birth, clergy in canonicals spouting the message of goodwill to all men, which was promptly shelved for the rest of the year, that made his soul sink. How did this absurdity start? Despite the best intentions of the Church (which he also had no time for) to keep the season holy, Christmas now started in September, cleared all sensible products from supermarket shelves, and created such an anti-climax in January most people went into social hibernation until it was time for Easter.

At a least the gaudy glitter and razzle-dazzle had not infiltrated the environs of the ancient parish church. It was peaceful here, as it should be. This land was sacred long before Christians arrived, and the building's foundations rested in ground that had witnessed millennia of rites welcoming the sun and mourning its loss at the onset of winter. The lives of whole communities had once depended on the whim of the season that was now used as an excuse to drink, party, and eat to excess.

The sky was filled with moonlight that cast a silver sheen on the ivy covered tombstones. A blackbird chimed, almost in time to the bell calling the faithful to six o'clock prayers, then fell silent at the warning hoot of an owl. A vixen, having spent a fruitful evening fossicking in the neighbourhood's restaurant bins, wended her way home to cubs that had long been weaned, yet were still unable to rootle out their own half eaten hamburgers. Nettles rustled with beetle devouring hedgehogs and Moon was just able to detect below the cacophony of the other wildlife the faint sound of snails munching through the petals of an expensive annual wreath laid on the grave of a much loved grandmother.

The church bell ceased to peal.

Moon took a long hazel wand from his coat and started to circle the church, stopping every now and then to tap its flint facade, the root of a tree or flagstone, at irregular intervals. Visitors to the cemetery paid little heed to his monthly ritual. It was a harmless, regular occurrence that had gone on for as long as they could remember and, like the moss cladding the bell tower, added an odd, pagan gravitas to the ancient stones.

As the overgrown path narrowed to accommodate the new community hall the brambles somehow failed to snag Moon's ankle length coat as he walked through them. The gaunt young man carried on as though the overhanging branches and nettles were not there, waving his long wand in the direction of the boundary they now concealed. The blackbird sounded a brief alarm then, as though realising it was only a friend, stopped. The hedgehogs did not fear his footfall either and continued to snuffle through the rotting autumn leaves.

Moon at last stepped out of the unkept thicket between the new extension and boundary to reach the north facing stones so covered with lichen his wand made no sound. Then on to the flint facade of the vestry recently cleaned of ancient encrustations where the tap, tap, tap could be clearly heard inside the Lady Chapel.

The curate watched from a slightly ajar window,

wishing the young man would go and have a decent
meal instead of circling the consecrated stones like
the mediaeval phantom that was rumoured to walk
the cemetery. She was a modern woman who did not
believe in spectres from the past, let alone that they
needed exorcising. The only impulse she had was to
invite the mysterious visitor with the wand inside and
fill him with communion wine and the sandwiches
prepared for the Sunday school party. Over the years
Barbara had tried to inveigle the young man inside
and find out who he was, but he always seemed to
disappear before she could reach him. Moon certainly
wasn't beating the bounds, or performing any sort of
pagan ritual she recognized. The mystery continued
to niggle away at her until the excited chattering of
children filled the community hall. Time to pour
lemonade and arrange the Nativity crib.

Tap: Mistress Chandler the candlemaker was laid
to rest here, her bones now intertwined with the roots
of a yew. Tap: four daughters and a son of Master
Bridgeforth, twice mayor and cloth merchant, lay
together against the foundations long sunken over the
centuries. Tap: below the flagstones of the bridle path
rested five families, 32 souls in all, poor weavers
starved during the harsh winter of 1316. Tap: the
sacrificed child under the first standing stone of the
original temple now lay deep beneath the crypt. Tap:
here, under the oldest remaining tombstone, lay the
wealthy miller and his wife; once both so plump and
long-lived, but remembered all the same. All souls
from a time the modern world had forgotten, yet still
lives punctuating a page of history that was this
parish. They could not pass into oblivion unremarked.

His ritual completed for another month, Moon
replaced the wand in his long coat and dissolved back
into the shadow of an ancient yew tree.

CAFÉ PECULIAR

The Oak Apple Tea Room with its Victorian sun
lounge nestled comfortably between a florist and
building society. At its rear was a large garden with a
rockery half submerged in a small river and, facing it
the main focus of the village, was the Jolly Toper. The
principal apprehensions of the residents here were
the river flooding and, in their minds just as
important, the spillage from the Toper's car park of
ancient bikers, hippy travellers and visitors from
anywhere east of Amsterdam. The village was a
Midsummer sort of place without the murders,
insular and wary of the great outside. It was content
in its quaint ways, even those bogus ones dressed up
for the tourists; after all, a yen could be just as
lucrative as a pound when the only thriving
businesses were a pub and the pedigree dog breeder
on the other side of the river.

Nicola had inherited the Oak Apple Tea Room
from a great uncle who had a sudden desire to start a
business rounding up camels in the Australian
outback, only to die of heat stroke within a month of
arriving. Being an animal lover, Nicola was relieved
at not having to wonder if the meat exported from his
failed company would be fed to the dogs in the
kennels on the other side of the river. She was a
warm natured young woman with a benevolent
outlook on the world. When her son Damian was born
and immediately accepted as his by her new
dependable husband, Alastair, life was complete.

Alastair Crum was a dapper, balding man who
looked a little older than his forty years. A true
gentleman, slow to anger and inclined to work things
out before reacting. Like Nicola, he trusted the world
to be just as reasonable and found it difficult to

comprehend that there could always be exceptions...

The High Street was clear apart from shoppers clutching bags full of sale bargains and trying to remember where they had parked the car. Nicola and three-year-old Damian seemed to be the only ones paying attention to where they were going. In the experimental pedestrian friendly area, the onus was on drivers to give way to people on foot, but there was always that exception...

Despite the efforts to console Alastair that the death of his young wife and child had been quick, he was too traumatised to accept sympathy. Months later, he was still numb with grief, automatically serving customers at the Oak Apple Tea Room because he knew that was what Nicola would have wanted. Then the case came to court. The young man driving the car only received a suspended sentence and loss of his licence for six months. Until then Alastair had not been confronted by the injustices of the real world. By the time it had sunk in that life was not so benign after all, it was too late to visit the killer of his family with a gun. The culprit had prudently changed his address and dented car, and the name he adopted would have confused the most diligent of private eyes. So Alastair was left with only the Oak Apple Tea Room and a void in his life for company, wondering, if pedestrian friendly areas weren't safe, where could anybody's loved ones walk without being mown down by the privileged majority who drove? Surely this world and the legal system he had always trusted was tragically out of kilter.

While Alastair's life was put on hold by his misfortune, the village won another award for being picturesque and the visitors increased.

Then, to the surprise of his neighbours, The Oak Apple Tea Room's sun lounge was converted into a fast food café and a patio that overlooked the river installed. Just as astonishing, Alastair suddenly developed an interest in collecting teapots. Customers assumed it was a way of dealing with his loss though, surrounded by so much eccentric pottery, they did feel that the Mad Hatter and March Hare might suddenly join them as they sipped their Earl Grey. Windowsills and shelves were crammed with teapots: the Houses of Parliament, Winnie the Pooh, Victorian grocers, post offices, armchairs, post boxes, Christmas puddings, fairy castles, clocks, elephants, fancy cakes, bouquets of flowers, quaint cottages - all possible subjects that could accommodate a spout and handle filled every nook and cranny of the old teashop.

Alastair was proud of his collection, frequently added to by appreciative clientele who didn't think his obsession odd and regular forays to craft fairs. The fast food cafe next door was for the less discerning and customers who fancied onion rings after sipping tea. While Carmen and Tracey kept the local schoolchildren and drivers of delivery vans satiated with burgers and chips, Alastair was free to potter about his teapot filled emporium and hold court with regulars who could remember the party there to celebrate the Queen's Coronation. After Carmen and Tracey had scrubbed down the work surfaces, topped up the condiments, and then left for an evening with the soap of choice, Alastair was free to tally the takings and watch the Jolly Toper opposite fill with customers.

After one particularly good day, Clive Newberry, the village's community constable looked in, wearing his grin to fit all eventualities.

He noted the pile of cash on the counter. 'Done well

today, Mr Crum?'

'Very well. My girls really excelled.'

'Best put it out of sight, though. A few suspicious looking bikers just turned into the Toper's car park,' he advised as though Alastair hadn't already noticed them.

'I will do that right away, Mr Newberry. Though my safe is so antique even I have trouble remembering how to open it.'

The constable touched his cap with an odd, old fashioned deference and crossed over the memorial to check on the pigeons still attempting to roost in the flue of the local pottery's kiln.

Alastair lowered the teashop lights, bagged the notes and coins, and deposited them in the back room safe. Before closing its door he removed a large envelope, which he took back to the counter. Glancing out to ensure that the local law enforcer's attention was elsewhere, he lifted his iPad from a cream cracker box and switched it on. There were more than usual special orders this evening, each one insisting on that special touch which made his blends so popular. They could take half the night. Alastair bolted the front door before going down to the cellar and setting out the requested ingredients. He would need plenty of caffeine to keep him going until the early hours.

Alastair returned to the teashop, pulled down the blinds and switched on the lamp over the side entrance. He took a cafetière of coffee to the largest table where he pulled out the contents of the envelope from the safe. There was a letter of thanks from The Campaign for Better Transport for his last donation of £5,500 and discreet form suggesting he could donate more directly from his bank account. If only he could, but the safest way was to send the cash by special delivery with a fictitious name and post office box number. The charity might have had suspicions about where the money was coming from, yet plenty of eccentric benefactors donated this way, and it gave the charity deniability if the money was found to be tainted.

Halfway through his second cup of coffee there was a discreet rap at the side door.

'It is open!' Alastair called.

Two leather clad bikers with helmets tucked under their arms quietly entered and pulled the door to after them.

When Alastair saw who they were his face lit up. 'Ah, Sebastian and Lola, what can I do for you?'

The burlier of the bikers sat opposite him. 'It needs to be quick. That copper's started to take an interest in the Toper's car park.'

Alastair waved his concern away airily. 'Oh don't mind him. He's only a boy scout. Heart of gold and brain of cotton wool. It's his baby-faced oppo you need to watch. Gimlet gaze and olfactory senses of a sniffer dog. Fortunately the real police force shows very little interest in our small corner of the world, and I very much doubt that they take the word of our community constables very seriously.' He studied the heavily tattooed features of the forty something visitor. 'Is it Lola's favourite tonight, then?'

'How well you know us.'

'Yes, a golden blend of toffee laced with white rhino.'

'That's my Lola.'

Alastair turned to the willowy, androgynous young man wearing a pearl earring and gold necklaces just visible against the rose coloured T-shirt under his leathers. 'Would you please hand me down Winnie the Pooh.'

Lola was familiar with the teapot and took it down from its high shelf.

'Ten grams will do this time, Alastair,' said Sebastian. 'Don't want her getting too high. She has to be returned to the family in mint condition.'

Alastair went to a display case and took out some silver scales. 'Still with the family, are you Lola?'

Once again, Sebastian answered for Lola as though possessive of every vowel she was likely to utter. 'The bikers would be happy to have her ride with the gang, but that father of hers threatened to report us for abduction. Bloody sure he has us followed. This Norton keeps cropping up out of nowhere. Bloke riding it doesn't try hard enough. His tattoos are always changing.'

'Oh dear. I shall certainly maintain a lookout for him.' Alastair weighed out ten grams of the tobacco/white rhino blend and sealed it in an envelope.

'Don't you worry Alastair. None of us would grass on you.'

'With the amount of grass in those teapots on the top shelf, what would we do if the real police did start to pay interest.'

Sebastian pulled out a much fumbled leather pouch. 'How much do I owe you?'

'To you, a special customer who would never grass, just eight pounds.'

Sebastian handed the exact money over. 'You're a gentleman and scholar, Sir. I'll be back for my mix in a couple of nights.'

As soon as the bikers had left, Alastair returned to the back room to remove a wad of £50 notes and special delivery envelope from the safe. He took them to the tearoom to jot down a brief missive, 'To save the planet from traffic, and bad drivers in particular.'

OLIVE'S ICEBERG

A red sun resentfully dawned through ribbons of leaden cloud and painted the ramshackle chalet on the beach in a lurid hue. The pebbles surrounding it gleamed malevolently as though soaked in blood. An old woman dressed in brightly coloured clothes came out to potter about the sea kale and dwarf broom of her garden. She cast a disapproving glower at the oppressive sun. At her frown the sky became filled with a glorious golden sunrise, the spangles in her skirt reflecting its light onto the flotsam and other bric-a-brac as she continued to rearrange it.

Satisfied, the old woman consulted a sundial made from a tangle of metal swarf filings. It was time to bring out the cracked plastic chairs. As an afterthought, she tossed a patchwork tablecloth over the ancient matching table to conceal the scratches and stains.

The old woman sat down to gaze at the marshland beyond the beach. A woman emerged from the early morning haze.

Olive was in her mid-50s, worn out by persistent diets and expensively dressed. She wore her smart outfit as though it was an infringement of the right to select something more comfortable; casual clothes to fit the woman-sized figure. Unfortunately she had made a "good" marriage which required the appearance of elegance, however much it may have gone against her instincts. It was impossible to return to the days of a youth filled with challenges to an authority she now sipped cocktails with, or wear trousers made from the discarded crushed velvet curtains run up when she had been a pecuniary student.

Olive was unsure how to approach the crumpled

old woman watching her and would have dashed back through the morning haze if she had not been beckoned into the ordered chaos of the beach garden.

On reaching the chalet, Olive become aware of the silence only broken by wind chimes and the waves gently lapping the nearby shore.

'No cars here?'

The old woman spread a gnarled hand. 'No need.'

'I'm Olive.'

'I know.'

'Are you really..?'

'Please sit down.'

Olive carefully negotiated the pieces of flotsam the sea had worn into fantastical shapes and wind chimes tinkling in a non-existent breeze. She gathered together the pleats of her tailored skirt and cautiously sat in the discoloured white chair facing the old woman.

'But are you really..?'

The old woman's face creased into a wry smile as she waved away the suggestion. 'No such thing.'

'I won't go anywhere until I know,' her visitor insisted.

The old woman leant forward, supporting her chin on spindly arms to look her in the eye. 'Just what were you hoping for, Olive? Something more spectacular? Greek chorus perhaps?'

Olive felt abashed. That's just what she had expected. 'Perhaps something more mystical, more awesome...'

The old woman laughed mischievously at the expectations of someone who had once challenged convention so vigorously. 'Flowing white beard and all that?'

'Perhaps.'

The old woman decided Olive had been tested

enough. 'Like some tea?'

That was more amazing than a choir of angels. 'You have tea?'

'Only Red Label.'

Olive hardly had time to blink when a teapot, two cups and saucers, jug of milk and sugar appeared on the patchwork tablecloth.

'We're not lactose intolerant yet are we?'

'Not yet,' said Olive. 'Having to contend with more serious matters at the moment.'

'Never underestimate the cow's revenge. Sugar?'

'No thanks.'

'It is all right to indulge yourself here. Nothing counts.' The old woman poured tea into the two dainty, chipped cups without hardly touching the Paisley pattern teapot.

Olive watched in rapt wonderment at her host's magical coordination and velvet sleeves which seemed to have a life of their own. 'You mean there are no rules?'

'No rules.'

'No panic attacks or ironing?'

'It's a drip dry dimension.'

'How do you pass the time?'

'Polish pebbles, drink tea, rearrange a few atoms in the Universe.'

Olive rose and took her cup to sip tea as she wandered the pebble garden filled with the bric-a-brac of a life she had almost forgotten; from the vases made with old 78 records to CDs spinning rainbow patterns on a mobile of wire coat hangers, and from the lavender bedside cabinet inlaid with paua shell to the ancient flatiron of student days. It was all here, the life she had sacrificed for self-indulgent comfort which lacked the pangs and euphoria that gave existence its meaning.

'You can see forever here,' she surprised herself by announcing.

'No such place as forever,' was the immediate response from the other side of the pebble garden.

Olive had become comfortable in this untidy otherworld, but self-awareness refused to let her relax. It gave her a sharp jab. 'Where am I then?'

'Everywhere... Nowhere...'

'Part of everything?'

'If you want.'

Olive had almost forgotten how much pantheism used to bother her. Then the recollections of a youth with multifaceted beliefs, fads, fashions and bold new futures swept back into her mind like the foaming tide of white horses lapping at the pebble beach. Her family no longer loomed large like a dense smog to suffocate the memories. They could not touch her here. All of the self-sacrifice, tension headaches and emotional blackmail could be seen for what they were... of no consequence whatsoever. Did Olive really squander so much of her life on self-delusion?

'You most certainly did.'

Olive turned, but the old woman had not spoken. She was still drinking tea and watching gauzy herring gulls merge with the brilliant sky laced with cirrus cloud.

Where had that hippy student taken the turning which could well have transformed her into a 22 stone hazard in the supermarket after the last diet failed, ignored by her self-centred, greedy offspring - a totally invisible 60 something? Better to become eccentric and annoy those she had wasted her life on. Or better still, remain that hippy, dippy student in a shack on some beach, rearranging pebbles and watching herring gulls.

She returned to the table and replaced her cup on

the patchwork tablecloth.

'Well?' demanded the old woman. 'Have you decided?'

For all the self-awareness, guilt still prevailed. 'But what about my family?'

'You can't go on taking the blame for the choices they make.'

'But they depend on me.' Only then did Olive realise that she had been the one who decided to become their emotional safety net, walking at a respectful six paces behind her offspring with comforting words and credit card at the ready. She felt like protesting at the futility of the life she had chosen for herself.

'But what else is there? Oblivion?'

'No such place as oblivion.'

'Tell me what happens?'

'Nothing you don't want.'

Olive took a deep breath. Perhaps the unknown, like the anecdotal stranger, was safer to know after all. New dimensions to experience, the Universe to ponder; assuming that thought still existed.

'Ready?' asked the old woman.

The chance would come again, but probably not on her terms. Better to take the plunge while the waters were still crystal clear. 'Ready.'

The old woman put down her teacup, reached up a weather-beaten hand, and tugged on an invisible cord.

The sunrise went out and the ensuing darkness became infused with intense light.

Desmond gazed apprehensively at the woman he had married and wondered at how major surgery had transformed her glowing features into wan papyrus. He wanted to share his concern with their children but, as usual, they were too busy bickering to pay attention. How had the bright, carefree offspring they had raised turned into such self-centred adults, rules by petty deceits and Facebook trivialities before their time?

He decided to break up their argument before the rest of the hospital heard it. 'Look you two, I'm going to need someone to be with your mother for a couple of hours each day while I check on the business. Miranda and Marcus can get too adventurous with the firm's management if not watched.'

Griselda turned to him as though his mental health needed assessment. 'What's wrong with Sandra doing it?'

'She's only paid to clean the house and has her own family to cater for.'

'Well hire a nurse.'

Desmond tried not to raise his voice. 'I don't want some stranger from an agency to have free run of the place. And she is your mother, for pity's sake! Is two hours so much to ask?'

'What's liable to happen to her in two hours?' David demanded. In matters of self-interest he was prepared to join forces with even his sister.

'You know what she's like. She could try to start cooking - or some fine thing - with no one there to watch her.'

'Well I can't do it,' Griselda said firmly. 'I've got three children to look after.'

His daughter had a point. If her 14-year-old was left to look after the younger ones, he would be out of the door to join his mates as soon as the BMW had left the forecourt, and his son worked 12 hours a day to try and pay off his wife's credit card.

It was too late for Desmond to regret wasting half a lifetime rearing the ungrateful brats when he and

Olive should have been cruising the world instead. Perhaps they could still do it; spend their children's inheritance on the indulgences of old age and leave them without a penny. Why hadn't he thought of that before? Olive deserved to at last be liberated from the matrimonial cage he had forged for her. They might even divorce, live in sin for a couple of years, and then remarry to spice things up.

Suddenly Desmond wanted to discuss the absurd idea with his wife. It would be glorious to see the reaction of their pompous children.

He gently shook her shoulder. 'Olive?'

There was no response.

'That's odd. The nurse said she should have come round by now,' Griselda announced as though discussing how long it took to boil a quail's egg.

'Don't worry,' David joined in. 'Mum is as strong as an ox.'

But Olive had stopped breathing. As Desmond had sat watching, listening to their children bicker, the life had slipped from her body without as much as a murmur.

Griselda's sudden panic attack brought a nurse running. She confirmed that Olive had been gone too long for resuscitation.

Desmond sat looking blankly at her body for an hour, thankful when David and Griselda had decided to leave. His daughter had been more worried about what to tell the children than losing a mother, and their son fixated on where she had put his shed keys just before being rushed into hospital.

In the clinical quietness of the private room, Desmond recalled what had attracted him to Olive. She had been carefree, guileless, and concerned for the welfare of all Earth's creatures. Perhaps it was time to realise some of those aspirations and sell his business. It was now worth enough to re-forest the slopes of the Brahmaputra - that would be a start!

Olive spread her arms, wanting to swim in the comforting strangeness of the saturating light.
    'Where is this?'
    'The rest of your iceberg,' the old woman told her.
    'My iceberg?'
    'This is reality. The part that would have turned your mortal mind if exposed to it.'
    'So what we knew as mortality was only the tip of what actually is?'
    'There would be untold collisions in the quantum universe if all mortals were exposed to it.'
    Olive assumed that she was now a quantum anomaly in an ocean of endless alternatives, and all she had to do was choose one - or all - of them.
    'Well let's go then!'
    'You can go for both of us,' the old woman told her.
    'How can I do that?'
    'Easily. I'm only the shadow of what you will now never turn into.'
    And, as Olive became one with the light, the old woman faded into infinity.

SEQUINS AND SAPPHIRES

Tiny turned a clod of earth over with the toe of his boot. There was the glint of gold. He was hardly able to believe his luck. Had such a minor cog in life's wheel as him, and only a cheap metal detector, stumbled across the hoard of the century? The young man was clenched by the same euphoria experienced when, for a split second, he believed his lottery number had come up. Should he phone the museum first, or dig a little deeper to be sure? He pulled off his gloves to excavate the suspiciously friable soil with fingers for fear of damaging a precious Saxon beaker or brooch.

Scumble barked.

Tiny glanced up. The last thing he needed was someone else to see that he had discovered treasure. But it was only a squirrel. The mongrel would ignore cats and rats, and run away from sheep, yet could detect a squirrel miles away. Tiny went back to work, using his fingers and a penknife to carefully scrape away the soil and daisy roots. It was somehow inevitable that the golden gleam would only turn out to be copper. Tiny's heart sank. If that had been in the ground for any length of time it would be tarnished green by now. Not only that, its burnished surface had been protected by a very modern coat of lacquer. Suddenly Scumble forgot about squirrels to find the object interesting. The dog started to dig.

It looked like rain and there was no point in trudging back through the mud without anything to show for it, so Tiny and his scruffy mongrel unearthed their find with the finesse of wombats grubbing up roots. All they had to show for the effort was a round copper container the size of a cake tin with a lid impossible to prise open.

The rain started to fall. Tiny pushed the find into his knapsack, picked up his metal detector and set off for home, not bothering to put Scumble on the lead as they crossed the field of sheep, knowing that he would keep well clear of them.

On the green velvet tablecloth in Tiny's basement flat the copper container with an exotic, embossed pattern looked strangely at home once it had been cleaned up. Most of the furniture and fittings had been donated by an elderly aunt, the one member of the family who hadn't ostracised him as borderline stupid and a hopeless underachiever. Aunt Veronica and Scumble were the only ones in the world who had much time for the 25-year-old. Ten employers, three girlfriends, and hundreds of job applications, and Tiny still hadn't found his niche in life. Part-time assistant to the groundsman at the local golf course was hardly a career; at least Scumble hated grey squirrels so vehemently he saved many a tree from being ring barked.

Although the container was barely tarnished, corrosion had sealed the lid on tight. Before reaching for a can of lubricant to free it, Tiny's imagination set to work to cushion the inevitable disappointment. There must have been a reason for someone burying it: stolen goods, perhaps? Or did it contain body parts which were meant to stay interred? Even Scumble, initially enthusiastic to dig up the container, now eyed it suspiciously. Would it be such a good idea to open it after all, or better to go and watch the Hellboy DVD?

'What do we do then, Scum? Open it?'

The dog cast its owner a sideways glance as though to say, 'Be it on your own head.'

His dog probably had better sense, but Tiny went to work with the WD-40 and a screwdriver all the same to work the lid free. Holding the copper container well away from his nose just in case there was an ear or internal organ inside, he opened it. Instead of a decomposing stench, the distinctive perfume of baby talcum powder wafted out.

For one dreadful, soul shuddering second, Tiny visualised the remains of a newborn infant, and then was reassured by Scumble's lack of interest. That dog had an acute sense of smell and would have been running up the walls by now if it had.

Tiny looked inside the container and began to remove boxes of sequins, diamante buckles, sapphire jewellery, and a pouch full of greasepaint, lipsticks and mascaras. Given Tiny's limited contact with the opposite sex, he had never seen so much makeup in one place. Most intriguing of all, packed tightly underneath the other items, was a blonde wig dusted with talcum powder, and below that some letters and postcards.

Once the contents were laid out on the green velvet tablecloth, it seemed amazing that so much could be crammed into a container hardly larger than a Dundee cake tin.

Tiny pulled the sapphire necklace and bracelet from their plastic sleeve and wondered at how the cheap jewellery reflected the light from his economy light bulb with such intensity. However inexpensive they may have been, it was inexplicable that no one wanted to retrieve them. Perhaps he should see if his Aunt Veronica wanted the costume jewellery; she liked anything that shone and had a Tiffany lamp with similar coloured glass. Then Scumble sneezed at the fragrance released from the letters tightly tied with yellow ribbon. It was more overpowering than the baby talc.

Tiny gingerly turned over each old postcard with

daguerreotypes of Edwardian ladies, Mucha poster designs and bawdy seaside cartoons, glancing at the elegantly scrawled script on the back of each. The missives mainly consisted of, "Have arrived safely", "Good wishes", and "Break a leg".

"Break a leg"? Tiny had a girlfriend with theatrical pretensions who used to say that. The messages were open and friendly so he had no compunction about reading through all of them. But the lavender envelopes were a different matter. These looked like love letters; love letters that had been buried in a copper container in a remote corner of the countryside. Perhaps he should repack the contents and return it to that hole in the field of sheep? But it was getting dark and still raining. He would do it tomorrow.

All evening the powdery contents of the tin lay on the green velvet tablecloth enticing him, even while he sat with his back to them, watching the TV and eating pot noodles. Eventually temptation defeated Hellboy, and Tiny returned to the table.

He was usually disinterested in the entanglements of other people's love lives, possibly because no one had ever confided in him about theirs. And it was not as if anyone would know if he had riffled through their personal billets-doux as these elegantly addressed envelopes came from a level of society a loser like him would never have access to.

Tiny carefully untied the yellow ribbon and pulled out a lavender coloured letter. At first glance the rapidly written message appeared more like an admonishment than commitment of fealty; this was confirmed as soon as he started to read.

'Well darling! That was a fine way to leave your lover, without a word of farewell, adrift on the turbulent sea of this ghastly production with a broken mast and frayed sequin bodice! You could have at least sent a postcard from the Rue due Perfidio!'

If there were any double entendres intended here, Tiny did not recognise them; he was a lost soul when it came to loose banter in the Dog and Trumpet. And the letter didn't begin with Dear 'whoever' either, just came straight to the point as though picking up after a rudely interrupted conversation.

'And leaving me with your screaming brat! You do know he scratched the bathroom cabinet trying to reach your stash of pot on the cistern!'

This was certainly no love letter.

Tiny took out another perfumed page.

'All right - don't reply! It's not as if I want you to take Adam back, and I don't suppose for one moment you can remember his mother's address, you callous worm!'

Tiny didn't bother to finish this one either and opened another rant from the furious Loretta.

'I suppose you're hoarding these letters for spite. Any other uncivilised reprobate like you would have at least had the decency to put "return to sender" on the envelopes'...

And another.

'I know that this won't bother you or that strumpet you ran off with, but your child had his operation today. They won't know if it's a success until Adam regains consciousness. So discuss that over your candlelit suppers with your expensive trash!'

Tiny stopped there. He had never been bombarded with so much personal drama in his lifetime and it was all too heady for him to take in at once. It made the young man wonder what it would be like to have a life filled with such emotion, either as the recipient being scolded by the passionate Loretta, or even as the deserted waif undergoing major surgery. It made him realise how much his existence had been lacking meaningful content from the cradle: a mother browbeaten by lack of opportunity and bullying father, and expectations that he would never amount to anything. Even the unfortunate Adam had a Loretta to shout on his behalf.

Having read the letters, Tiny now faced a dilemma. Despite all the disorganised slovenliness of his single existence, the young man unaccountably had that germ of empathy lacking in his drinking pals. Even the ones with families were mostly mouthy, fumble fisted incompetents when it came to recognising the feelings of others. He often cringed at the things they said about their girlfriends and wives. Whoever had buried the letters so long ago would have probably enjoyed their company. Tiny also felt concern for the young boy who underwent major surgery: did he survive? Did Loretta survive? At last he was confronted by a real, heart wrenching conundrum at odds with a life that had consisted of one blunder after another.

'What do I do, Scumble?'

The mongrel just gave him the "Isn't it about time you fed me" look.

Tiny jotted down the address at the top of the letters and repacked the copper container's contents, hesitating to once again examine the sparkling sapphire necklace and bracelet which had been so carelessly tossed in as if an afterthought. No - they couldn't be real; probably glass! He returned the jewellery last before covering it with some crumpled tissue paper that had wrapped the present his last girlfriend had hurled back at him for calling her by the wrong name, before pushing on the lid. Then he opened a tin and fed Scumble.

The next morning Tiny caught a bus. It took a 90

minute ride and half-hour walk to reach 20, Cherry Garden Lane.

The address was not the elegant townhouse he had expected. It was at the centre of a village that had become a suburb without loosing its rural charm. Some grass verges were filled with wild flowers and others planted with pansies and polyanthus, and the terraced cottages should have housed milkmaids and shepherds. The road reminded Tiny of the Victorian countryside idyll his aunt Veronica had hanging in an ornate frame over her mantelpiece.

A local resident glanced at the visitor and his scruffy dog with curiosity and forbearance, as though accepting he had a good reason to be there and, when he reached the front gate of number 20, a large woman bustled up the path towards him as though marshalling competitors at the local gymkhana. She wore a delicately flowered print dress under an ancient duffel coat that looked as though it had been left in the farmyard overnight. Tiny was probably one of the few people unlikely to register the incongruity

'Oh, they must have gone on ahead some while ago,' she called, then noticed Scumble and hesitated as though seeing the potential sheepdog in the mongrel. 'Who were you looking for?'

'Loretta,' Tiny offered nervously, intimidated by the suddenness of her familiarity. Many people seeing a scruffy stranger at a neighbour's gate would have assumed he was a vagrant and called the police.

The wind left the sails of the galleon bearing down on him. 'Oh yes - of course. You obviously don't know, do you?'

Tiny wondered what faux pas he had made now, so took the copper container from under his arm in the hope it wouldn't make matters worse. 'Got something of hers.'

The large woman unexpectedly pulled out a tissue and wiped away a regretful tear at some failing on her part. 'Oh, I'm so sorry. She's not here.'

'Then perhaps Adam could take it.' Tiny didn't know what else to say. Despite his best intentions, had he managed to do it yet again - blunder in at the wrong moment?

'Oh, I must be too late now, so you might as well come with me,' the woman suddenly decided. 'My name's Hattie.'

'Mine's Tiny.'

'I'm afraid your dog will have to go in the back.'

She led them to a mud spattered four-wheel-drive, opened the rear door and ordered Scumble into the compartment behind a safety screen. To Tiny's surprise, his mongrel obeyed without a whimper and sat gazing at the back of their heads as Hattie drove to a crematorium. Tiny was now convinced that he should have returned the copper container to its hole and forgotten about it.

As they entered the drive of The Willows, which was lined by commemorative plaques he decided to remain silent, an art learnt during a life of hard knocks and having a father fast with his fists and slow with words, especially after a few beers. Hattie parked in a discreet area set aside for grieving relatives, and then grasped Tiny's arm to bustle him to where a deceased's ashes had just been scattered. She released him to dash over to a tall, statuesque woman wearing deep purple and a heavy veil, and threw her arms about her.

'Oh, I am so sorry, Loretta! I really wanted to be here, but the foal was a breech birth...' she gushed.

'It's all right, Hattie. It's all right. It's a beautiful commemorative plaque. He would have loved it.' Loretta raised her veil to observe Tiny. The face was

ageing but, like her ankle length dress, immaculate.
He had never encountered a woman so imposing or
heard a husky voice so seductive.

Tiny involuntarily glanced at where the ashes had
been scattered.

'He would have died much earlier if it hadn't been
for Loretta,' Hattie announced simply.

'I'm... sorry,' Tiny stammered.

Loretta smiled reassuringly. 'Why bless you dear,
there's no need for you to be sorry.'

Tiny held out the copper container. 'I don't know if
this is the right time...'

'Well, well, what do we have here?' There was a
suggestion in her tone that she had already guessed.

Loretta put on an elegant pair of reading glasses
and watched keenly as Tiny prized the lid open.

'I really didn't mean to, but I read some of the
letters. That's how I found out your address.'

By the change in Loretta's expression as she saw
the container's contents, it was unlikely what he said
had registered. Her heavily mascaraed eyes lit up as
though she had rediscovered her lost youth. She
delicately pulled away the crumpled tissue paper to
reveal the sapphire necklace and bracelet.

'Oh, dear God! Hattie! Hattie! Just look!' Loretta
held up the necklace and the gems sparkled in the
sunlight.

'Ain't real, is it?' Tiny asked tentatively.

'Oh you sweet thing, of course it's real! These are
the long lost jewels from time when we were younger
and had money to squander.'

'They must be worth a fortune,' added Hattie.
'Though I was always in two minds about whether
they actually existed. Loretta always knew how to
beguile the gallery with tall stories.'

Loretta sighed wistfully. 'But I would never have

dared wear these on the stage. I so wanted him to see
me in them one last time.'

'Well put them on now then. He might still be
watching.' Hattie took the necklace, lifted Loretta's
veil aside, and fastened the jewels about her satin
collar.

Tiny handed her the bracelet and she pushed it
onto a long, silken glove.

'He was such a fool, spending all that money on
me, then forgetting where he hid them.'

'He hid them..?' Tiny stopped.

'Why yes. He had to go abroad for several weeks on
business and took them with him to get the jeweller
to adjust the chains. While he was out of the country
he was taken seriously ill. He only received the
wretched letters in this tin some time later. We had
argued before he left and I was convinced that he had
found someone else. I had no idea how badly the
illness had affected his mind. When he did eventually
come back to the UK, he believed I never wanted to
see him again. He had always been such a
muddleheaded creature before the illness, like his son
in many ways.'

A tall young man standing nearby had been silent
until then. 'Not so muddleheaded I wasn't able to
track him down to that nursing home.'

Loretta extended her hand to the good looking 20-
year-old. 'This is Adam, his son.'

'And this is a Loretta, my mother. I only knew my
father towards the end of his life - I don't think he
ever realised who I was.'

Until then, Tiny thought he had grasped the
intricacies of the situation; now confusion must have
been written in his face. 'Then... She's your mother?'

'Oh yes, in everything but blood. Poor Justin
couldn't remember who my real mother was. But I

was lucky. Loretta raised me. I now belong to the
family of best drag queens in this county.'

THE BLOOMING OF BROCK'S BOG

The track from Meadow Hill Farm twisted and plunged its way down through the gorse bushes until it ran alongside the green, bubbling soup known as Brock's Bog. Here the path had become overgrown through disuse. The effluvium of the quagmire kept away any creature with olfactory senses; even ramblers avoided the short cut it offered to the picturesque valley beyond. It was a curiously still place, as though the very breeze held its breath sooner than pass over the fetid water. The only movement was made by rising bubbles of methane.

So there Brock's Bog lurked, oxygen-less, barely liquid and totally unloved.

As this mire straddled the boundary between two counties, neither council was prepared to own it. A speculator did suggest it should be drained and turned into a recreation park, but no civil engineer would guarantee that the stench could be removed from the ground and the planning application was shelved. It was hardly surprising that the alienation towards Brock's Bog triggered rumours that it was haunted. Nobody was quite sure why or by what, but there had to be some explanation for Nature creating this monstrous feature which could deter the most ardent toad and rot any gossamer seed having the audacity to land on its pea green crust.

Alice was a survivor. To her, the meaning of life was nothing more profound than an answer in some inane quiz thought up by a tabloid sub editor jaded by the daily excess of bare boobs and libellous trivia. Kevin, her husband, could finish the Times crossword in five minutes yet, if he did comprehend what their humdrum existence was about, he certainly never

gave Alice a clue. He was cantankerous, controlling,
self opinionated and, because he had letters after his
name, could argue down any lesser mortal who didn't
share his point of view. Neighbours ducked behind
their neatly clipped hedges or suddenly scrutinized
some point of interest in the opposite direction when
they saw him coming. Alice, the fun lover, and Kevin,
the redundant accountant, were totally mismatched
in a relationship that breeds terrible dependence.

Both daughters had tried to persuade their mother
to take the rest of her life off and have some fun
before it was too late. Their father found out and
banned them from the house, knowing that it would
be difficult to persuade anyone to bale out of a failed
marriage surrounded by their screaming young
broods in the public arena of a Tesco cafeteria. And
what if she did leave him? The only work experience
Alice possessed was as a part time seed packer in the
local nursery; hardly a vocation guaranteed to give a
55-year-old woman an instant mortgage. She
certainly wouldn't have moved in with either of their
daughters and their rowdy children.

Kevin became increasingly bitter about his
overqualified unemployability and resentful of the
small wage Alice brought in, and when she started
working full time he suspected that she was up to a
lot more than packing seeds of cabbage and forget-me-
nots. Infidelity couldn't have been further from his
wife's mind - the man she already had was enough for
one lifetime, but that green-eyed monster had its
twitching nose above the parapet. Sometimes Kevin
would cut short his afternoon at the wine bar to
secretly watch his wife laughing with the other
packers as they came out through the ornate nursery
gates. What had they got to laugh about? No doubt
some private joke at his expense. Women were like

that, you couldn't trust them out of your sight.

Then Kevin started to follow Alice during her lunch hour.

The more friends he discovered she had, the more jealous he became.

He searched the drawers of her dressing table and kitchen cupboards. He found that the tin marked "flour" contained wholemeal biscuits; the one labelled "spices", out of order and crumpled household receipts, which so offended his book keeper's brain it might as well have been infidelity. The less he was able to find, the more suspicious he became. It was almost a pity he wasn't there to see the head nurseryman secretly hand Alice that small, unmarked packet of seeds. Kevin would have immediately deduced that she was going to leave for South America with a Latin gigolo to start up her own cannabis farm. In fact, the contents of the small envelope were almost as illicit - the seeds of the water hyacinth which had clogged so many waterways of the world. These were of a new hybrid commissioned by a water filtration company who wanted to use the plant to mop up the impurities from polluted water. The idea was simple and economic, and the roots of this variety could be pressed into chipboard without the risk of the furniture made from it sprouting at the first hint of moisture.

Alice's request for the seed was quite innocent and only for a small unsightly pond stagnating at the bottom of her garden. She had bordered it with a few rocks to give a home to the frogs and hoped the water hyacinth would conceal the eyesore. For fear of the small packet being lost in the clutter of till receipts, sticks of makeup, envelopes, elastic bands and three different purses filling her handbag, the seed packet was placed in her blouse pocket for safe keeping. As usual, Kevin searched the contents of his wife's handbag for incriminating evidence as soon as she was busy in the kitchen and, as usual, found nothing but the customary jumble of items; certainly nothing to indicate that Alice would not be returning home the next evening.

Kevin waited a day before telling his daughters that their mother had disappeared, and two more before phoning the police. He knew what conclusion the neighbourhood would come to, and the inquiries of the police only confirmed their suspicions that Alice had at long last plucked up the courage to pack a suitcase and leave.

At the loss of the only person who knew how to operate his rewind key, Kevin became indolent; sleeping late and eating less. Persuaded that Alice had left of her own free will, the police made a token circulation of her photograph then put her at the bottom of a missing persons' list.

The more the well-meaning tried to draw Kevin out of his gloom, the faster he slipped back into his shell like a misanthropic tortoise. He had always nagged Alice about her easy gong attitude to housework and now had the opportunity to keep things as immaculate as he wanted. He should have been glad to lose her, cashed In his shares and moved to the Riviera, or even attempted to open a small accounting business. But then there would have been no one to blame when things went wrong. With Alice, the world had always revolved around him.

Eventually Kevin had to admit that the unremitting failures in his life hadn't been her fault after all. Then the worst fate that any mortal could inflict on themselves engulfed him... blame.

The sun beat down on the crust rapidly breaking up on Brock's Bog. Leaves appeared - large, bright green leaves. They punctuated several square metres of the quagmire and soon sat like large islands surrounded by clear water. Nobody would have noticed if a rambler, who had taken the wrong turning, had not mentioned their appearance to the landlady of The Three Horseshoes. Her daughter Amy, a keen botanist, cycled down the track from Meadow Hill Farm every two or three days to keep watch on their progress. She realised that they were a rare species of water hyacinth and, anxious to see them in flower, kept their location to herself.

After several weeks, steeples of bloom pushed up from the rich, green mattress of leaves. The white petals were much larger than wild water hyacinths' and attractively edged with purple fringes. Amy knew she was obliged to report their appearance. Hybrid or not, any botanist was regretfully aware that this plant had the potential to destroy all the hard work of the volunteers who had recently cleared the local canal system. Water managements had draconian ways of dealing with cloggers of drainage systems and munchers of indigenous trees, however attractive or endearing. The coypu had learnt that to its cost.

Amy was just taking out her mobile phone to make the fateful call when something that looked as though it had been coated in ancient shellac bobbed to the surface of water that had not yet been colonised by beautiful blooms.

The body was impossible to identify and the police were unable to establish how long it had been submerged in the bog. Prior to the sudden arrival of the water hyacinths it had been free of oxygen and capable of preserving a corpse for centuries. It could have been a Viking for all they knew, but carried

wounds that looked too much like foul play for them
to readily surrender it to any archaeologist.

Even though the water hyacinth hybrid had
turned the fetid quagmire of Brock's Bog into a tourist
attraction, the water authorities insisted that it had
to go. Their efforts to find out where the plant had
come from were almost as intense as the
determination of the police to discover the identity of
the body. They were eventually persuaded by their
pathologist to hand the remains over to the
archaeologists impatiently waiting to carbon date
them.

Marion Watson, Landlady of The Three Horseshoes,
vigorously polished another glass. 'I reckon it's one of
those ramblers, meself.'

Annie, her barmaid, stopped counting the day's
takings. 'Really? I'd have thought ramblers would
have more sense.'

'Not some of the ones who come in here. I don't
think half of them would know north from south if
they had a compass stapled to their shorts.'

Annie gave a nervous laugh. She had no idea about
the identity of the body in the bog, but did know
where the flowers had come from. Those seeds may
have been intended for a stagnant frog pond at the
bottom of her suburban garden but how much better
they had looked, briefly cloaking that deplorable
landmark which residents at one time wouldn't admit
to being in their county. And, after all, they had
brought to the surface the Iron Age sacrifice which
was now the star turn in the local museum.

GREEN AMBER

Benny was one of, what he believed to be, a dying breed - a librarian. Whenever there was a book sale at his branch to make room for more computers he ensured he had first pick of the most desirable volumes. His apartment walls crammed with books, many of them not yet available in electronic format, were testament to a life long devotion to the printed word.

Benny was halfway through his weekly routine of dusting the rare volumes of Jane Austen, Holinshed, and Guttenberg, (Enid Blyton, Agatha Christie and Charles Dickens, however collectable, were usually only attended to once a month), when that envelope dropped through his letterbox. One glance at the expensive stationery and handwriting told him that it meant trouble. Commonsense insisted he toss it straight into the recycle bin; appalled curiosity told him to at least open it first.

For all its ostentatious letterhead and expensive watermarked paper, the letter only contained a brief note.

'Typical of Max', thought Benny, but the invitation he made was unsettling enough to spur him to remove the small jewel box secreted in the bottom drawer of his bureau. Inside it was a large piece of polished, green amber and a note in that same careless handwriting, 'A green eye for a jealous lover!'

The accusation still made Benny recoil. It had been totally unjustified and cruel, and from a partner he should have left long before it had been sent. The painful recollection made him reach for the photo album kept on a top shelf with other best forgotten correspondence. Out tumbled the faded Polaroids and postcards that had fallen from their worn paper

hinges. They brought back the glorious, traumatic
memories of Caribbean cruises, Monte Carlo casinos,
carnivals in Río, and stunning sunsets over Angkor
Wat. Max had the money for those adventures and
Benny had been happy to tag along, even though it
often meant being second best to some pretty steward
or croupier. There was no antidote for reminiscences
that potent.

Benny put away the duster and photo album, and
secreted the green amber in his jacket pocket. There
was no need for an umbrella; the weather was set fine
for the rest of the day and the address was only a tube
ride away, just far enough to be out of range of
surveillance cameras Max had no control over.

The mansion in the leafy green suburb stood
secluded in its own grounds. It must have cost
millions; millions Max had somehow managed to hang
on to during his 20 year stint in jail. It was ironic that
after so long fencing stolen goods and drug dealing,
his lover should have been convicted for a murder he
didn't commit.

Benny stood before the huge ornamental gates,
unsure whether to announce his presence. Once
committed it would be impossible to back out.

But the decision was no longer his when that
dreadfully familiar voice, gruff with cigar smoking,
announced from the intercom beside the wrought
iron, 'Come in, Benny. I've been waiting for you.'

The lock on the gates clicked and they swung open
like Art Nouveau teeth of hell. There was no escape.
Benny walked up the long, tiled drive to the porch
more suited to a hotel. Ostentation had always been
Max's weakness, so unlike Benny's modestly tidy
world.

It would have been no surprise if the ornately
carved front door had also swung open automatically,

or at least been opened by a young man dressed in
mauve satin. Instead, there stood Max, robust, tanned
and with the gleaming gold toothed smile that never
aged. Benny should have been repelled by the
arrogance of the man, so confident that he would
accept his invitation, and wanted to resist the
welcoming bear hug, only to hate himself for not
wanting it to end.

Gathered up by the man's overbearing bonhomie,
the small librarian was swept through the opulent
hall which opened out into a conservatory Kew
Gardens would have found useful.

'I'm really glad you came, Benny, really glad.'

There was no accusation in Max's tone, but Benny
could still read the man's nuances, even after all this
time. He hadn't been able to bring himself to visit his
old partner in prison during the 20 years he had been
incarcerated there. How could he explain to Max that
he didn't want to get involved with all the pimps,
fences, and drug dealers he spent so much time trying
to avoid before his lover had been convicted of
murder? Just one visit and he would have been back
in the charismatic thug's clutches, his trusted liaison
with the criminal world outside. However much
Benny had once been devoted to the man, it wasn't a
future he could face. And, by the luxuriousness of
Max's mansion, it seemed that he had found other
"aides-de-camp" to carry out his business. So why had
he been summoned to the demon king's castle? There
was nothing he could offer Max. The
uncharacteristically coy glances the large man was
casting in his direction were even more unsettling. He
had never held anything back before: when the crime
lord had blurted something out the whole criminal
underworld were aware of it. So what dreadful
prospect had his old partner allowed himself to walk

into?

'Drink, Benny?'

There was no choice but to take the ageing bull by
the horns. 'Just why did you need to see me after all
this time, Max?'

'I've got some decent sherry.'

'Max!'

As if unbalanced by a glancing blow, Max slumped
onto a couch and rolled a half filled whisky tumbler in
his hands as though it was too hot to handle. 'Twenty
years inside gives you time to think, Benny.'

'Think about what, Max?'

'We were really close, weren't we?'

'Yes, we were until...'

Max swigged back his whisky then unsurely got up
to fitfully pace between the exotic orchids and ferns. 'I
know, I know! It was my fault. I should never have
sent that note.'

'Green amber for jealousy.'

'I was drunk. I just thought you didn't like me
being with Poppy. I know you were never jealous of
any of the little tramps I picked up. You always knew
none of them would last.'

'The final one didn't last long at all. You and Poppy
were only together for a couple of weeks.'

Despite his bumbling attempts to be conciliatory,
Max detected the edge in Benny's tone. This librarian
was no longer the simpering doormat he remembered.
'No Benny! You don't really believe I murdered that
little trollop, do you? '

Benny went to the drinks cabinet and poured
himself a whisky. 'Well, somebody did.'

Max wondered when his old partner's taste for fine
sherries had been replaced by one for hard spirits. 'It
wasn't me, Benny.'

Of course it hadn't been Max. He could get rid of

gold diggers and blackmailers without resorting to murder.

'So what am I doing here?'

Max's booming tones were lowered to a whisper. 'I missed you, Benny. I didn't realise how much until you weren't there. I didn't treat you well. I don't need pretty boys any more. They just bore me. I need someone my own age. Someone I can trust. Someone I can talk to.'

Benny could hardly believe what the man was saying. 'You want me back?'

Max nodded. 'Come and live with me, Benny. I promise things won't be the same as before.'

The librarian in Benny was dumbfounded; the pragmatist insisted that it would mean no more getting up at six to open the doors for the vagrants who used the library as a daytime doss house, and being polite to little oiks whose minds were so muddled by their mobiles and iPods that they thought Lenin was the leader of a 90s pop group.

Benny took a swig of the whisky in a way that suggested it hadn't been the first of the day. 'So what business are you in now Max?'

The large man was immediately defensive. 'I run a clean business, Benny - I swear. Property renovation. Don't even rent it out - just sell it on.'

No, Benny had never taken Max for a Rackman; everything between that and a drug cartel boss, perhaps. He might have actually been telling the truth. Perhaps he would never need to encounter the low life that swam in the pond Max used to rule like a corrupt Poseidon. But there was one thing about Max that Benny could be sure of - he was a convincing liar.

'Another drink Max?' Benny reached out to take his glass.

Max drained the whisky and handed it to him,

knowing better than to press his old partner for an immediate answer.

Benny took their glasses to the drinks cabinet. Before he refilled them, he involuntarily touched the green amber in his pocket; the real reason he had decided to come.

'Who do you think poisoned Poppy, Max?'

The question took him by surprise. 'No idea, he was a sweet little thing really. Could have been one of those other jealous tramps trying to muscle in. They were all stewards, handling food and drink.'

Benny smiled wryly. 'Yes, Poppy had been a sweet little thing.' He handed Max a tumbler of whisky. 'Might have been a real chance to find out if it hadn't happened in the middle of the Atlantic. You were the obvious culprit, so into the brig you went.'

If the crime had occurred anywhere else, Max's fixers would have spirited him away before the law arrived. But this was on an American cruise liner and all the bodyguards and appeals to Uncle Sam's benevolence counted for nothing. The best Max could do was cut a deal so he served his sentence in the UK. It was a glorious irony that the only time Max really needed an efficient copper it was on a US cruiser in the middle of the Atlantic.

Benny raised his glass. 'To the future, Max.'

'To our future, Benny.' Max downed his whisky in one swig.

Benny watched his slightly addled ex-lover with analytical curiosity. Had he made the right decision? The man was overbearing and repellent in many ways: now he was older and, after a life of excess that would have wrecked the health of a younger man, his faculties would no doubt shut down one by one.

Then the penny dropped. Max was ill. Seeing him after so long, the slight slurring of words, unpredictable reactions and uncharacteristic undercurrent of fear suggested senility. Benny was being sounded out as the last person on the planet who might be prepared to nurse him to the end. Did the librarian really want to spend his approaching retirement nursing this monster of a man, who would probably become aggressive as soon as he lost any ability to reason? Not to mention the risk that Max would find out who had actually killed Poppy.

The young steward's death had been a mistake, of course. Benny had been smitten by the bright, innocent youth. He regretted that his overpowering partner had got between any romantic attachment that might have developed while they both waited for the other to make a move. But Poppy had no idea what Max was really like. How could someone so inexperienced have anticipated his violent mood swings? In an ideal world Benny should have saved the boy that trauma by escaping with him to make a new life together. And why did Poppy's eyesight have to be so appalling without his contact lenses? If it hadn't been, he would never have picked up the glass of whisky intended for Max instead of his own ginger cordial. Fortunately it only had Max's fingerprints on it.

Unfortunately, Poppy died.

The only positive thing to come out of the wretched business was Benny's independence from the thug. Once released, physically and emotionally, he had no choice but to build the life that most suited his withdrawn nature and modest needs. Jealous lover? Yes. But only because Poppy, the ideal life partner, had been snatched from him.

It took longer than anticipated, but Max at last started to clutch his stomach in agony. He was bound to blunder about and bellow, so Benny watched from the conservatory door as the large man tried to reach for his mobile. It obviously still hadn't occurred to him that the only person he truly trusted would poison him.

Finally, over went the glass table, covered in blood spattered vomit, before Max crumpled to the floor strewn with rare orchids.

The one good thing about working in a modern library was the degree of electronic competence required. Benny found the security terminal in the property's surveillance room and deleted everything from the last two hours, giving himself another thirty minutes to put on examination gloves and remove all trace of his presence, leaving no fingerprints, footprints or threads to link him to his visit. He even found the combination to open the security gate into an alley at the rear of the mansion, through which he silently left.

Benny had genuinely shared an emotional bond with the criminal baron, but it had been suffocating, fearful, unpredictable and stultified the life he really wanted to lead. He should have been racked with remorse. Instead he felt light-headed with relief.

Free at last, Benny walked all the way home along the Thames, now able to savour the luminous light that Whistler had seen reflected on its water.

REVENGE AND CHIPS

The chips didn't seem to be as greasy as Joyce remembered them, but that had been over 25 years ago. At least the same old raincoat still fitted her and she was still able to squeeze into the narrow cubicle seat from where she used to watch the world go by without it staring back.

The windows would have dripped with condensation if they had not been wiped with detergent to allow a clear, albeit streaked, view across to the boutique. Young trendies used to buy overpriced clothes hardly able to cover their embarrassment there; now it was a new age store where not so young people in hair extensions considered papier-mâché ornaments and tunics made in Nepal.

Joyce sliced through a fish finger with her fork and dipped it in the puddle of tomato ketchup. A lifetime of being determined to fit into that same old raincoat until the day she died had made her forget how moreish cheap food was. However, the tea hadn't changed and was still corrosive enough to polish brass. She dragged streaks of ketchup through the sauce of the baked beans with her knife and marvelled at how badly the two colours blended. At least meals here were still served on plates and not in polystyrene as though the management wanted the customers out before they started to wonder what went into the food. Gabriella, the current proprietor, was proud of the plates she filled for the early morning cabbies and porters who had a citation run up in appreciation, though a heart clinic would have preferred the local council to close her place down.

Joyce stiffened her resolve and once more ploughed into the chips. Half a lifetime of sensible eating had shrunk her stomach and determination wavered when the apple crumble and custard arrived. On the aisle table next to hers a pair of hungry eyes also analysed the dessert, instinctively sensing it would go begging at any moment. Joyce picked up the dish and, without a word, pushed it towards her neighbour, adding the spoon as an afterthought just in case he was desperate enough to tackle it with those long nailed fingers.

A gnarled hand gave a half salute. 'I thank you, Mum.' The dessert was rapidly fed through a grizzled beard so unkempt it was a wonder he could remember where his mouth was.

Joyce lightly buttered a piece of white bread, placed six chips inside it and nibbled her way through them. It was amazing how much better things tasted when in a sandwich, even one made of bread with the texture of finely sliced cotton wool.

A small, wrinkled woman hugging a much used carrier bag came in and sat opposite the bearded man. Without looking up, he rubbed his spoon clean on a discarded paper serviette then pushed it with the remaining apple crumble across the table to her.

Common sense nagged Joyce not to do it, but Gabriella was looking straight at her over the counter unit crammed with Danish pastries, sausage rolls and sandwiches. 'A cappuccino, please.' Joyce pointed to the adjoining table and discreetly flourished a £20 note. 'And whatever they want.'

The proprietor wasn't fazed. Given the number of late night revellers still feeling good about the world, who passed through in the early morning, the occurrence couldn't have been that unusual.

'That is most kind of you, my dear.'

For a moment, Joyce wasn't aware that the voice had come from the small, creased woman.

'It's okay.'

Within half an hour the couple had devoured between them two all day breakfasts, four rolls, two cheese sandwiches, bread and butter pudding and three mugs of drinking chocolate. Joyce could remember being that hungry; fortunately not very often.

The bearded man jabbed the air with a teaspoon. 'Much better than hostel food.'

'Kitchen there's got cockroaches,' agreed the woman. 'This place is clean.'

Joyce made an effort to sound interested and was surprised how easily the ability still came to her. 'Have you far to go then?'

'Only round the corner. We have to be in by eight. Could lose the beds otherwise.'

Joyce half smiled. The couple seemed content enough so there was little point in bestowing sympathy on them as well as a meal.

'What do you do for a living, my dear?'

Again, the small woman's question was as unexpected as her plummy voice.

Joyce had to collect her thoughts. 'I, er, pickle things.'

'For a living?'

'Oh yes. Great market for it. You can make chutney with almost anything, you know.'

'What do you pickle then?'

'Sweet corn, celery and capers, cherries in rum, bamboo shoot pickle, walnut, carrot and mango chutney. Oldest profession in the world. Humans wouldn't have survived if they hadn't learnt how to pickle food.' Joyce was aware enthusiasm was running away with her tongue and stopped herself from going into the manufacturing processes involved.

From under his outgrowth of hair, the man had
fixed her with a beady look. He leaned over and asked
in a conspiratorial whisper, 'Then what are you doing
in a dive like this?'

Joyce edged closer to the smell of tobacco and
carbolic soap to tell them, 'I'm celebrating.'

'In here?'

'25 years ago to the day I set up my business. Over
this very table,' she tapped the chipped Formica, 'I
took my first order for Mr Levison's delicatessen.'

'He's gone now, you know,' the woman observed.
'Son didn't want the business so he sold up and went
into wholesaling. Old place is a betting shop now.' She
turned to watch a young man in chauffeur's livery
enter, buy a mug of tea and go to a table by the door.
'Hope he doesn't leave that Rolls there long. Kids
round here haven't got any respect for paint work.'

Joyce gave a small giggle at some private joke.

The old woman guessed what it was and wondered
why the chutney entrepreneur had limited some
important occasion to a plate of Gabriella's fish
fingers and chips. 'Going on somewhere else then?'

'In a moment,' Joyce told her. 'I had to eat
something to line my stomach first in case I end up
drinking more than is needed to be sociable. And I
have to give a small speech.'

'Family affair then?'

'They wouldn't come.'

'Why not?'

'I made it clear I was leaving everything to
charity.'

The man spluttered on his tea as the comment
struck a chord.

The woman laughed. 'Simon's family tried to
persuade him to give them power of attorney. They
wanted to put him in a home so they could get their

hands on his property. So he gave it all to a seaman's
retreat.'

The businesswoman in Joyce couldn't see the joke.
'But surely ... Wasn't that pulling the rug from under
his own feet?'

'Now they leave him alone. He's better off in a
hostel than some old people's institution. You know
what they do to you in those places?'

Joyce nodded.

'Fill you full of tranquillizers and leave you on the
loo,' the man added. 'When I go I want it to be sudden
and with a bit of dignity.'

The woman pulled back several sleeves to reveal
an expensive watch. 'We had better get going, Simon.
You don't want to sleep in the underpass in this
weather.'

The man muttered a few things as he fastened one
of the cardigans under his greatcoat. He rose and
gave a nod of gratitude to Joyce.

The woman took his arm to steady him. 'Thank
you for the meal, my dear, it was most appreciated.
Perhaps we will see you again some time?'

'If my family doesn't succeed in having me
committed to an institution in the next few years, you
probably will. This chipped Formica holds fond
memories.'

As they left, a small man bustled from the kitchen
and cleared away the plates before Joyce could leave a
tip under hers.

She waited until the cafe was empty, apart from
her waiting chauffeur, before easing herself out of the
cubicle seat to remove her old raincoat which she
handed to him. Joyce straightened her shot silk
business suit and touched up her face with lipstick
and powder.

'How long will it take to get there, Tony?'

'About five minutes, Madam. The theatre traffic has slackened off.'

'Good. Drive to the emergency exit. I don't want to meet the press. As soon as the takeover is announced I want to get away fast before my brother knows what hit him.'

'Surely he must have suspected that you were the one buying up shares in his company, Madam?'

'Not him. He's too arrogant to think I would dare, and the dealers were careful to cover any tracks that could lead back to me.'

'Your brother can hardly be prepared for it.'

After a brief wave goodbye to Gabriella they stepped outside where they didn't need to keep their voices down.

'Good. Nor was I when he assumed control of my company 15 years ago because I was naïve enough to trust him with the accounts.' An icy smile crossed Joyce's face. 'It's nice to have a loving family, Tony, but never trust them with your money. If I'd known that to begin with I wouldn't have had to spend ten years building up a second business so I could regain control of my original company.'

And Tony knew all too well who would be first to go. At least his job as a chauffeur to the owner of one of the world's largest pickle manufacturers would be secure.

*

Also published by Dodo Books

Science Fiction books by Jane Palmer

Babel's Basement
The Planet Dweller
The Watcher
Moving Moosevan
Nightingale
The Kybion
Hunder
Duckbill Soup
The Aton Bird

***

Fiction

Bald Wendy

***

Short Stories for Older,
and Not Quite so Old, Children

(Written under the name of Dandi Palmer)

9 781906 442293